# I REALLY
## want
## the cake

# I REALLY want the cake

Simon Philip                    Lucia Gaggiotti

**SCHOLASTIC INC.**

There's a smell I can't ignore.
It's wafting through the kitchen door.
It's time for me to find out more.

I think . . .

. . . it might be cake.

It's on the table sitting there.
I cannot help but stop and stare.
And now I'm really quite aware . . .

. . . I think I want
the cake.

The decoration's just so neat.
That icing looks like such a treat.
It smells so chocolatey and sweet!

# I REALLY want the cake!

I want it now, and though I'm small,
I'm sure that I could eat it all.
But Mom has written in a scrawl . . .

I'd be a fool to disobey.
To eat the cake is **NOT** okay.
And maybe if I go away . . .

. . . I might forget the cake.

I'm really trying to be strong.
To eat it would be very wrong.
I've wanted it for so, so long!

# I must . . .

. . . forget the cake.

That thought has made me rather glum,
and all I want is one small crumb.

My mom says no, but I say yum.

YOU MUST NOT

I'm going BACK for cake!

It's still there waiting, nicely placed
for me to have a little taste.

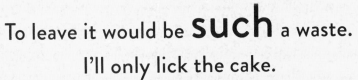
To leave it would be **such** a waste.
I'll only lick the cake.

# Oh my, oh my! What a delight!

Somehow the lick became a bite.

I can't control my appetite.

Just one more slice of cake.

I know I've not been very wise.
And what I've done I can't disguise.
I might have to apologize . . .

. . . because I ate the cake.

Oh, silly me! What have I done?
I'll have to make another one.
I guess it could be kind of fun.

I've never **baked** a cake.

I need some eggs! I'll start with six.
It's sure to be a tasty mix.
There's nothing that I cannot fix!
It's **easy** making cake!

I'll whisk and beat and stir and shake
until my arms begin to ache . . .
Oh no! That wasn't meant to break!

It's **hard** to make a cake!

My gosh, the **mess!** It's everywhere.
It's up the walls and in my hair.
When Mom sees this she'll faint, I swear.
It's chaos making cake!

Hi, Mom, I've come here to confess.
I'm sorry if I've caused you stress.
And yes, I've made a lot of mess . . .

# . . . but hey, I've made you cake!

For Morgan, Iris, Derek and Angela,
for all your love, encouragement and cakes!
— SP

All my love to my nephew, Alessandro,
who is sweet like chocolate!
— LG

Text copyright © 2017 by Simon Philip
Illustrations copyright © 2017 by Lucia Gaggiotti
First published in the United Kingdom in 2017 by Templar Books

ISBN 978-1-338-71608-5

10 9 8 7 6 5 4 3 2 1      20 21 22 23 24

Printed in the U.S.A.   40
First printing 2020